Tale
of a
TADPOLE

Orchard Books, 95 Madison Avenue, New York, NY 10016

Manufactured in the United States of America
Printed by Barton Press, Inc.   Bound by Horowitz/Rae
Book design by Jennifer Browne

10 9 8 7 6 5 4 3 2 1

The text of this book is set in 14 point Veljovic Medium.
The illustrations are watercolor paintings.

Library of Congress Cataloging-in-Publication Data
Porte, Barbara Ann.
Tale of a tadpole / by Barbara Ann Porte ; illustrated by Annie Cannon.
p.   cm.   "A Richard Jackson book."
Summary: Francine and her family watch as their pet tadpole Fred
gradually changes into what they think is a frog until Grandpa tells
them Fred is a toad that should be living in the backyard.
ISBN 0-531-30049-8. — ISBN 0-531-33049-4 (lib. bdg.)
[1. Tadpoles—Fiction. 2. Toads—Fiction.] I. Cannon, Annie, ill. II. Title.
PZ7.P7995Tal 1997 [E]—dc21 96-53890

Tale
of a
TADPOLE

by BARBARA ANN PORTE
illustrated by ANNIE CANNON

ORCHARD BOOKS

NEW YORK

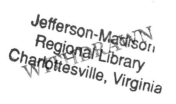

For Evan Porte Thomas
and again, of course, for Julia
                                    —*B.A.P.*

To the memory of my mother's beloved toads,
potatoes, and potato-print toads;
and to Doug T., one of the young folk who
scientists hope will "sign up"!
                                    —*A.C.*

In this fish tank lives a tadpole named Fred.

Every day Francine feeds him fish food and waits for his feet
to come in. It's what they told her to do at the nature center.

"It could take a long time," Francine's mother says.

"You have to be patient," says Francine's father.

"I've heard of frogs turned into princes just because some princess kissed them," Francine's older sister tells her.

Of course she means in fairy tales. "Have you tried kissing
Fred?" she asks.

Francine ignores her. But every day she watches Fred
to see if something's happened.

Weeks go by. . . .

Fred looks a little larger.

Then one day, as Francine is filling up the tank with water from the pond, she sees something.

"Quick, quick, come look!" Francine calls to her family.

They come running.

"Frog legs," Francine's mother says. "Back ones, anyway."

"It's a step in the right direction," says Francine's father.

"Funny-looking toes for a prince, though, don't you think?" asks Francine's older sister.

Francine ignores her. But every day she watches Fred to see if something new has happened.

Days go by. . . .

Fred's tail looks longer.

Then one day, as Francine is adding stepping-stones to the tank, she sees two bumps behind Fred's head. At bedtime, Francine looks again.

"Quick, quick, come look!" Francine calls to her family.

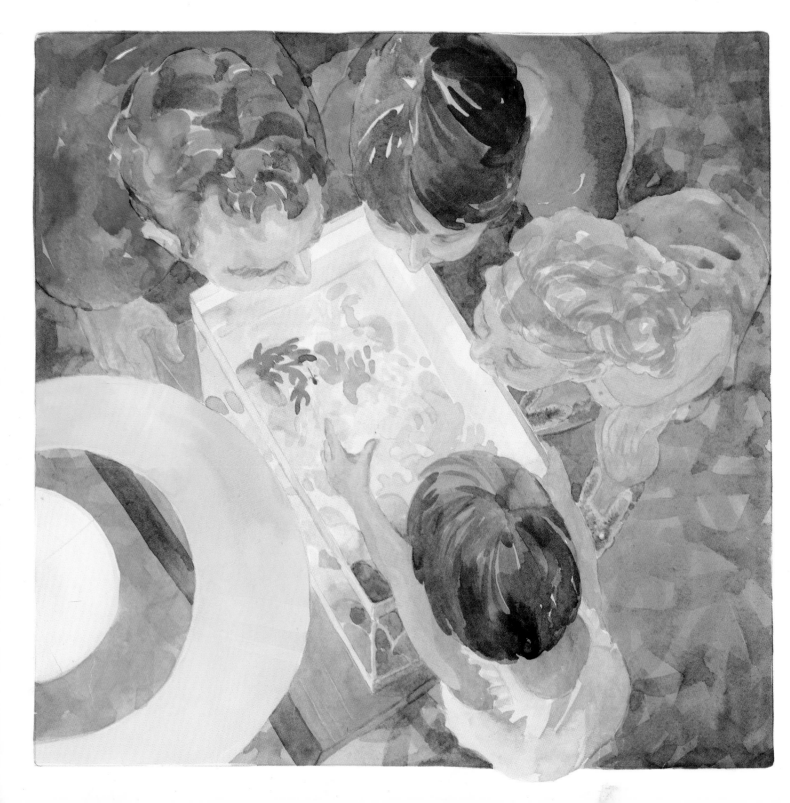

They come running. They're just in time to see one bump pop out an arm. The next day, Fred has two.

"That looks almost like a frog now," Francine's mother says.

"A froglet," says her father.

"Or a princelet with a tail," says Francine's older sister.

Francine ignores her. But now she gives up feeding Fred. All
the nutrients he needs are stored in his tail. Francine knows
this from the nature center. But every day she still watches

Fred to see what more will happen. Day by day, this does: Fred's arms and legs get fatter, Fred's eyes get bigger, Fred's mouth gets wider. Only his tail keeps getting shorter.

"Don't worry. Frogs don't need tails," Francine tells him, unworried.
Then for the next few days, Francine forgets to watch. Finally she
remembers. She rushes to look. But where can Fred be?

Francine stares and stares. A tankful of water is all that she sees. Then, suddenly, "Quick, quick, come look!" Francine calls to her family.

They come running. All of them stare.

There on the top stepping-stone sits a small frog with barely a stub for a tail. He's staring back at them.

"Well, well, well. Just look at that Fred," says Francine's mother.

"Congratulations," Francine's father says.

"It's hard to imagine any princess ever wanting to kiss him, though, isn't it?" asks Francine's older sister.

Francine ignores her. She hurries off to catch insects to feed Fred.

A few days later, Francine's grandparents come for a visit. Francine shows them her frog.

"His name is Fred," she tells them.

"Hi, there, Ted," her grandpa says. He's a bit hard of hearing.

"That Fred certainly is a good-looking toad," says Francine's grandma, who hears fine.

"Toad?" says Francine.

"Right," says her grandma. "Your Fred is a true toad if ever
I saw one. A toad is a kind of land frog."

"How can you tell?" asks Francine.

"Pardon me, what did you say?" asks her grandpa, turning
up his hearing aid.

"How do you know Fred's a toad?" Francine shouts.

"No need to shout. I can hear you fine now," her grandpa says. But he's glad to explain. "See how dry his skin is, and how bumpy. See

how short his legs are. If Ted were a true frog, his skin would be
smoother and wetter. His legs would be longer. His back toes would
be webbed more. He'd be slimmer. True frogs live in ponds. True
toads live in woods and backyards."

"Your grandpa and I once had a pet toad in our backyard," says Francine's grandma. "It lived there for years. It caught plenty of spiders and insects, believe me."

"If I were you, I'd put that Ted in the yard and let him catch bugs too," Francine's grandpa says.

"His name is Fred," says Francine. Still, backyard living sounds good to her. She's getting awfully tired, anyway, of having to catch so many insects to feed him.

Therefore, that same day, very carefully, Francine takes Fred from the tank, carries him out to the yard, and sets him on the ground.

As she watches, he hops away, but not too far. Using his hind
legs, he digs a hole in the dirt and backs into it. Fred looks up

at Francine and blinks. Then he flicks out his tongue and catches
a small fly. Fred pushes in his eyes and swallows it.

"It's a good pet that doesn't need too much attention," Francine's mother says after dinner that evening.

"Or shed," says Francine's father.

"I wonder if kissed toads turn into princes too," says Francine's older sister.

Francine ignores her. But Francine's grandma says, "Oh, I'm sure they do. But you just try and find a princess nowadays who'll kiss one."

"Princess, schmincess," says Francine's grandpa, his hearing aid turned up. "I'd say the story's ended when everyone lives happily ever after."

Well, then, that's that.

All of them do.